The Very Hungry Hedgehog

Rosie Wellesley

PAVILION

Isaac the hedgehog had slept through
the winter, snug-safe and curled up
under the leaves.

"Time to wake up!"
shouted Starling.

The ngry g

First published in the United Kingdom in 2018 by
Pavilion Children's Books
43 Great Ormond Street
London
WC1N 3HZ

An imprint of Pavilion Books Company Ltd.

Publisher and Editor: Neil Dunnicliffe
Assistant Editor: Harriet Grylls
Art Director: Lee-May Lim

ISBN: 9781843653530

A CIP catalogue record for this book is available
from the British Library.

10 9 8 7 6 5 4 3 2 1

Reproduction by Tag, UK
Printed by Imak, Turkey

This book can be ordered directly
from the publisher online at www.pavilionbooks.com
or try your local bookshop.

"Wake up, dozy friend,
come on out and see spring!"

"Is this spring?" muttered Isaac,
"It's so sludgy and wet."

Isaac crawled out from his long-winter bed.

"That worm looks delicious,
Can I share, feathered friend?"

Starling looked up from her breakfast.

She laughed:

"Ha ha HA! Look at you!

Bad hair day for hedgehog!"

And still chirping and smirking, off the bird flew.

'Bad hair day?' thought Isaac,
feeling hungry and hurt.

She wouldn't look good if she'd
slept all the winter.

And she was his friend!

Well, he would find his own food.

So he upped and he
offed and he marched
into the world.

A nose poked out of a hole in the ground.
It slunk through the mud, warty and squat.

"Are you hungry,
too, Toad?"

Isaac spotted
a beetle.

"Watch me, see how it's done."

Hedgehog leant forward and stuck out his tongue.

"Oh Toad!

You gluttonous wretch!
If you had asked I would have shared!"

With hurt feelings and a hungry belly
Isaac squelched on.

"But here is a slug!
Sleek, slimy and fat.

So slug-a-licious.

Breakfast at last!"

"So tasty,

so juicy,

and..."

swOOsh

"Oi Heron, not fair!"

Isaac was ever so hungry.

His friend Starling had mocked him.
The toad was just mean.
The heron had snatched.

Why couldn't they share?

Life had been better in bed.

Isaac stopped.

He looked around, and he finally saw.
'This is Spring', he thought.

'Which means slugs, hatching bugs,
some fat grubs, and more.
There must be food enough for
a feast for us all.'

Then he found it. An earwig.
Best breakfast of all!

His eyes rounded,
mouth watered,
jaws opened…

"Hooooo

"wwwwlmph!"
cried out Fox.

And

"Ohhhhhhhh!"
went Hedgehog.

As he fell back to earth he knew Starling was wrong.

'I don't have hair, I have SPIKES! Not bad hair day, GOOD SPIKE DAY!'

and he bounced on the ground.

The fox looked quite scared.

"Don't touch me," he said,
"that really hurtshh."

"I'm not food!"

laughed the hedgehog,

"So don't try it again. But get
up – look around."

"Spring is finally here,
and with help you will
find there's enough food
for us all,"

For Coco, who has shared so much. x

Sorry for being
mean. Starling x